WATER,
WATER

WATER, WATER

Cary Fagan

ILLUSTRATIONS BY Jon McNaught

tundra

Text copyright © 2022 by Cary Fagan
Illustrations copyright © 2022 by Jon McNaught

Tundra Books, an imprint of Penguin Random House Canada Young Readers, a division of Penguin Random House of Canada Limited

Library and Archives Canada Cataloguing in Publication

Title: Water, water / Cary Fagan, Jon McNaught.
Names: Fagan, Cary, author. | McNaught, Jon, illustrator.
Description: Written by Cary Fagan and illustrated by Jon McNaught.
Identifiers: Canadiana (print) 20200415972 | Canadiana (ebook) 20200416006 |
ISBN 9780735270039 (hardcover) | ISBN 9780735270046 (EPUB)
Classification: LCC PS8561.A375 W37 2022 | DDC jC813/.54—dc23

Published simultaneously in the United States of America by Tundra Books of Northern New York, an imprint of Penguin Random House Canada Young Readers, a division of Penguin Random House of Canada Limited

Library of Congress Control Number: 2020952416

Edited by Lynne Missen
Designed by John Martz
Printed in China

www.penguinrandomhouse.ca

1 2 3 4 5   26 25 24 23 22

Penguin
Random House
tundra   TUNDRA BOOKS

For Sophie and Rachel and Yoyo and Elena

1

Floating

Even before Rafe opened his eyes, he knew that something wasn't right.

It was the kind of feeling he'd had on waking up in a strange hotel room or on a friend's fold-out sofa during a sleepover. Only this time Rafe knew that he was in his own bed. Same mattress, same sheets, same pillow. But even so, something was different.

He opened his eyes. Yes, here was his room—desk, chair, dresser, cork bulletin board, heap of clothes he hadn't put away by the door. The only thing different he could see was that the bulletin board was hanging crookedly. Had he accidentally nudged it in the night on the way to the bathroom?

And then he realized what was different.

He was *moving*.

Not just him, but his bed. His bed and, presumably, his room. It was a subtle movement, a gentle rising and then sinking again. It wasn't jarring or scary, but it was definitely noticeable. What was causing it? An earthquake? It didn't feel like one, at least not like the way he imagined one would feel. It felt more like—well, like lying on an inflatable raft in his friend Russell's pool as it moved gently on the water.

The movement continued. Okay, this was definitely weird. Rafe sat up. He ran his hand over his face to make sure he was fully awake. He could tell that it was daytime by the bars of light seeping in between the blinds covering his window.

He stood up.

"Mom?"

"Dad?"

No answer.

"Buddy?" he called. "You there, Buddy?"

Buddy was Rafe's dog. He was half beagle and half poodle—small, smart and curious. Buddy always responded instantly to the sound of Rafe's voice, but there was no sound now. Could they all be in the backyard, the basement or the garage?

Rafe (whose full name was Raphael Blumenthal, but everyone called him Rafe) knew exactly how far it was from his bed to the window. Two and a half long steps. He knew everything about the room where he'd slept his entire life. His bed had a wooden headboard upholstered in blue and white squares. Before it he'd had a smaller, lower bed with a gate so he wouldn't fall out. And before that he'd had a crib. The world that he knew started from this room. It radiated out from here like spokes in a wheel, to the rest of the house, the front and back yards, the street, the park and school and beyond.

He got out of bed and took those two and a half strides to the window. He put his hand on the blind's pull-cord. Of course, he knew what he would see. His room was on the right side of the house, near the back. He would see the back of the Cardoso house next door and part of the Cardoso's deck with its deluxe barbecue.

With one quick pull, Rafe raised the blind. But he did not see the end of the Cardoso house. He did not see the deck with its barbecue.

He saw blue.

Blue water, with little whitecaps. And above it, blue sky.

The view was wide open. Lots of water—not merely blue but a blue green—stretching to the horizon. And lots of sky—pale with long, high, wispy clouds—rising as high as he could see. No wonder he could feel his room moving. The house was *floating*. On an *ocean*. Just the night before, his house had been sitting on the earth, a thousand miles away from any large body of water. But it was definitely on the ocean now.

These thoughts came to Rafe in a strangely calm manner. Perhaps that was because the movement he felt was so gentle. But underneath that calm was something else. Underneath it was panic. Fear. He had to push it down so as not to break his calm.

Rafe swallowed and took a breath. The first thing he had to do was find his parents. They would know what was going on. His parents knew everything, didn't they? From the window to the door of his room was three and a half steps. He turned and took those steps to the door, pushed aside the clothes with his foot, and opened it.

Water. Lapping right up to the edge of his room. There was no hallway, no bathroom, no rest of the house. A little wave splashed onto his bare toes. He quickly shut the door.

"What the—?"

Rafe spoke out loud. His heart pounded. There was no hope of calming down now. His room—and only his room—was floating on the ocean like a little box. The rest of the house was gone. His parents and his dog were gone. The street was gone. Everything was gone except water and sky.

And then he heard something.

Barking! His dog wasn't gone! He'd recognize Buddy's voice anywhere.

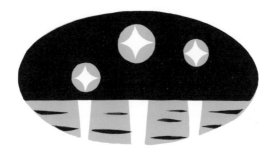

2

A Better View

Rafe rushed back to open the window. "Buddy! Buddy? Where are you, boy?"

The barking started again. Rafe leaned out the window, turning his body to look all around. And there was Buddy, up on the roof of his room (actually the other side of the ceiling), poking his head over. As Rafe watched, the dog darted desperately forward, one of his paws slipping past the edge so that he collapsed onto his stomach before pulling back again.

"Stay, Buddy! Don't fall off. I'll get you somehow."

Rafe retreated back into the room. What did he have that would allow him to get onto the roof so that he could bring Buddy down? The answer came to him right away: the ladder!

Under his bed was a fire-escape ladder. His parents had put it there and had shown him how to use it. It was meant to hook over the window ledge so that Rafe could climb down from his second-floor room and escape. But he wasn't on the second floor anymore and, besides, now he needed it to go *up*.

He pulled the metal ladder out from under the bed. It was made from hollow aluminum and was easy to hold by the sides and maneuver out his window. He raised it upward with the hooks at the top. It was hard to keep the ladder from tilting away, but he held it straight up with effort and, when the hooks were just past the edge of the roof, he lowered it so that they hooked on.

The dog whined and yipped as it pawed at the ladder. Buddy was a smart dog, but he didn't know how to climb down. Rafe would have to go up. The only problem was that Rafe didn't like heights.

He didn't have a *fear* of heights, exactly. He just didn't like them much. He wasn't keen on climbing trees or crossing bridges. But now he had no choice. He decided to get dressed quickly, before Buddy got too impatient and tried to come down by himself. He went to the pile of clothes and pulled out underwear, a T-shirt and a pair of jeans. He found his basketball shoes by the door. Then he hauled himself onto the window ledge.

It wasn't so easy getting onto the ladder. He had to push himself out the window without letting go and grab onto the ladder from the other side. Then he had to pull his feet off the window ledge and onto the ladder's bottom rung. The wind ruffled his hair. Below, the water lapped against his room. He took one step and then another, making sure his foot was secure before moving up.

"Get back, Buddy, stop that!"

The dog was scratching at the ladder. The top of Rafe's head reached the edge of the roof. As Rafe moved up higher, the dog began to lick his face. "Hey, give me a chance to get on," Rafe said, pulling himself onto the roof.

He lay on his back, afraid that he might tumble off the edge. The dog put his paws onto Rafe's chest and licked him again. "Good dog, good boy," Rafe said, roughing up his fur. He put his arms around the dog and hugged him hard.

"I guess I better get up," Rafe said. First he got onto his knees. Seeing that he was far enough from the edge, he slowly stood up, keeping his feet apart to steady himself. He had a better view now and turned in a circle so that he could see 360 degrees around.

And what he saw was more water. No land at all. Not even far away on the horizon. Not even an island.

"Where did everything go, Buddy?" Rafe asked. "Where are the houses, the skyscrapers, the mountains? Where are Mom and Dad?"

But all Buddy could do was rub against Rafe's legs. Rafe shaded his eyes. He saw that the sun was on its way down, which meant that he hadn't gotten up in the morning as he had thought but in the afternoon. Perhaps even days had gone by. He kept looking, kept turning slowly, and gradually he began to make out some other objects on the water. But they were too far away to identify. Were they boats? Other rooms like his own? Maybe they were pieces of debris from a giant storm. But had he really slept through a storm fierce enough to wash everything away?

Rafe stayed up on the roof for what felt like an hour, hoping that something might come into view. But it began to get dark, and the air got cooler, and he was worried about climbing down the ladder if he couldn't see. So he picked up Buddy and, holding the animal to his chest, made his way back down the rungs and through the window into his room. He pulled in the ladder.

Rafe was relieved to get back inside. It was all that was left of the world he knew. The dog seemed glad, too, jumping up onto the bed and nosing under the blanket. Rafe went into his bottom drawer where he kept a stash of goodies. He took out a Choo-Choo bar for himself and a block of sponge toffee for Buddy, knowing that chocolate could make a dog sick.

"I guess this is going to be our dinner," Rafe said. He unwrapped them both and put Buddy's on the floor, where he gobbled it up. Rafe ate his bar more slowly, chewing thoughtfully and gazing out the window. It was a good thing that his water bottle was in the room. He took a sip and then put some in the top for Buddy.

His room was getting dark and without thinking he flicked the light switch. Nothing happened.

"Of course," he said to the dog. "No electricity. No light, no heat. Good thing it's May. Also, no internet, no phone." He felt a new rise of panic and told himself not to get carried away. "Things are going to be okay, Buddy. I mean, I'm just a kid and you're a dog. We can't be expected to figure out what happened, or how we're supposed to live. Doesn't Mom always say that things look brighter in the morning? I'm sure everything will get straightened out tomorrow."

He got into his pajamas, climbed onto the bed and slipped under the covers. Buddy lay down beside him and within minutes was sleeping, his side moving slowly up and down. Rafe hadn't been up very long but he felt exhausted. Still, he didn't go to sleep right away. It was completely dark now except for the stars visible through the window. He looked at them for a long time.

3

Scoop

When he stirred in the morning, arm around his sleeping dog, Rafe thought that he had just woken from a dream in which his room floated like a boat on the sea. But as he sat up, Buddy yawning next to him, he began to doubt. Immediately he went to the window, the blind still open, and saw the sky (more cloudy today) and the vast expanse of water (more dark green than blue) and knew that it hadn't been a dream at all.

Buddy got off the bed and started moving in tight circles, his back legs ridged. Rafe knew what that meant. "Hold it in, old boy," he said and put the ladder out. Then he picked up the dog and started to climb.

"Stop squirming. I might drop you," Rafe scolded, but the dog only wiggled more as he moved up rung by rung. When he reached the roof, the dog jumped out of Rafe's arms, almost knocking him off the ladder.

"In the corner, Buddy, go in the corner." Rafe pointed and, being a smart dog, Buddy obeyed. Rafe himself had to pee, so he checked the direction of the wind and then got as close to the edge of the roof as he dared. He would need to find something that could work as a shovel to clean up after the dog, and after himself too.

It was while looking down at the water that Rafe saw an object, or rather several objects, bobbing on the surface. They were close together, forming a ragged line in the water, and they were drifting toward the room.

"Buddy! We've got to get down. Come on!"

He grabbed the dog and hurried down the ladder again,

swinging them both through the window. "We need something like a net," he said, looking around. "Wait, I know!"

Rafe went to his closet, opened the door and began pulling stuff out of the jumbled mess. How many times had his mother asked him to get rid of things he didn't need? But now it was turning out to be a good thing that Rafe was a pack rat. He tossed out a snowsuit, football, an airplane with a missing wing. "There it is!" he called, grabbing his lacrosse stick.

Rafe had been on the school lacrosse team when he was ten, but he hadn't played for two years. An ancient game invented by Indigenous people, lacrosse required a long wooden stick with a net-like pouch at one end for catching a ball. The stick was perfect. Rafe went over to the window and looked down. Yes, the shining metal cylinders were still bobbing near his room. He was pretty sure what they were—cans of food that had lost their paper labels in the water. And now he could see there were dozens of them. He pulled a chair over to the window, climbed onto it, and while Buddy growled anxiously next to him, Rafe reached down as far as his arms

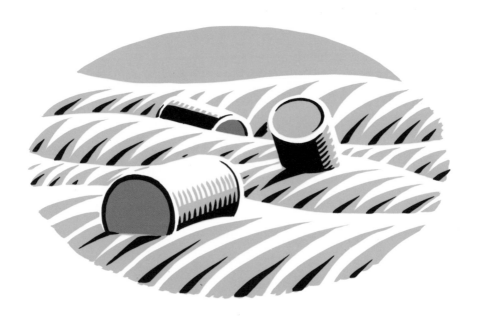

could stretch. He dipped the pouch end of the lacrosse stick and made a sweeping motion, catching up a can.

"Yes!"

He brought up the dripping can, pulled the lacrosse stick back into the room, and dropped the can onto the floor so that it rolled under the bed. Buddy barked at it. Rafe went fishing for another, caught and dumped it, and went back again. He got ten, then twenty, thirty, his arm growing sore, but he managed a few more before the cans drifted too far away, or else his room did, it was hard to tell, but either way the floating "school" of cans was now out of reach.

Rafe spent the next while finding the ones he had caught—under the bed, the desk, the chair. Some had landed on the bed, others in his pile of clothes. He wiped them with a T-shirt and neatly stacked them in the basket where he was supposed to put his dirty laundry.

"I wish that I knew what was inside those cans, Buddy," he said. "But whatever's in there is better than nothing, that's for sure. Too bad they aren't the kind with a pull tab. We need to figure out how to open them."

"Really, Rafe," he said, imitating the booming voice of Mr. Bellweather, his teacher at Smulder Street Middle School, "you mean to say that you don't keep a can opener in your room? You know, in case you find yourself floating in the ocean."

"Well, Mr. Bellweather," he answered himself, "I guess I'm just not as prepared as you always told us to be."

"Be resourceful, young Blumenthal. You did learn that, didn't you?"

"I sure hope so, Mr. Bellweather. Wait a minute, I do have a screwdriver."

"Now we're getting somewhere."

The screwdriver was at the back of the skinny drawer under the desktop. He had used it to put together a radio-controlled airplane that crashed the first time he tried to fly it. A screwdriver wasn't usually used to open a can, but Rafe looked around, found a large stone that he'd picked up on a hike, and banged on the handle of the screwdriver so that the steel tip would go through the top of the can. But it only dented the metal, so Rafe used the stone to sharpen the end of the screwdriver as if it were a knife. He tried again and this time it neatly pierced the can. He did it over and over, moving the screwdriver a little each time, until the lid had been sheared off. Then he picked it off with his fingers, careful not to cut himself on the sharp edges.

"Kidney beans. Not exactly our favorite breakfast, Buddy. But plenty of protein."

In the same manner, he opened another can. "Peaches in syrup! A main course *and* a dessert. Not too shabby, I'd say."

Buddy, excited by the smell, barked his agreement. Once more Rafe looked around his room. He noticed the two ceramic bowls with faces painted on them that he'd made at Camp Weeping Willow. He took them down from where they were displayed on the wall, poured half the beans and half the peaches into each, and then spread the syrup over both. Buddy ate his in about seven seconds, but Rafe, using a plastic ruler as a spoon, made himself eat slowly. As he chewed, he stared out at the cloudy sky and wondered where his teacher, Mr. Bellweather, was at this moment. He was pretty sure he knew where Smulder Street Middle School was. It was underwater. Maybe Mr. Bellweather was underwater too. Maybe every other human being was underwater. Including his parents. Were his parents—he could hardly let himself even think it—dead? Did they experience something terrifying and painful before life was over for them? Would Rafe never see his mom smile at him in that way that made him feel so special? Would he never hear his dad laugh as if Rafe was the funniest person in the world? Would he never again feel safe and protected and cherished and loved?

A tear rolled down Rafe's cheek. He was about to begin full-on bawling when something—or rather some*one*—drifted into view.

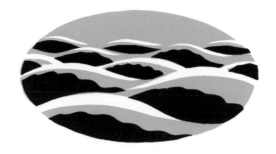

4

Johann Sebastian Bach

It was a woman.

She was wearing one of those fancy black suits—a tuxedo, Rafe thought they were called—only it was all dirty, as if she'd slid down a muddy hill. She was sitting on a wooden crate. The wooden crate was at one end of a wide wooden door. Each end of the door was resting on a floating barrel.

At the other end of the plank, a cello lay on its side.

The woman was sitting on the crate with her elbows on her knees and her chin on her hands. She didn't look very happy, but that seemed understandable enough. She had her eyes cast down and didn't seem to see Rafe standing at the window of his room.

"Excuse me?" Rafe said.

The woman looked up. Her face changed from depressed to surprised. "Dio mio!" she cried, standing up. "Un altro essere umano!"

"I think that's Italian. I'm sorry, I don't understand."

"That's okay," the woman said. "It's good to see you. I thought I was all alone in the world."

"Me too."

"Would you like a chocolate-chip muffin? This crate is full of them."

"Sure! And I can throw you a can, only I don't know what's in it. Do you have a can opener?"

"I have a pocketknife that's pretty strong. That might work."

The woman took a muffin wrapped in cellophane and, aiming carefully, tossed it through Rafe's window. He got a couple of cans and threw them one at a time. The first hit the crate but the second fell short, splashing into the water. The woman had to lean down to grab it.

"Are you a musician?" Rafe asked.

"Yes, a cellist. In an orchestra."

"Do you remember what happened?"

The smile disappeared. "I don't know exactly. You see, we had a performance in another town. In the school gym. Terrible acoustics, but what can you do? I got a lift home with the second violinist, had a cup of herbal tea, watched some late-night TV and went to bed. And when I woke up—here I was. My whole house was gone. You see these barrels? They had been used as flowerpots beside my entrance. And this big door that I'm standing on? I have no idea where it came from. And look! By some miracle my cello came through without a scratch. Crazy, don't you think? But I couldn't survive without it."

"I couldn't survive without Buddy," said Rafe. "Buddy's my dog."

On hearing his name, the dog leaped up into Rafe's arms. He looked out the window at the cellist, whimpering a little.

"He wants you to pet him. He's very friendly."

"It would be very nice to pet a dog. I wish I could reach."

At that moment a larger wave moved past. It caused Rafe's room to rise. It caused the barrels to begin turning away. The woman's face looked rather concerned as her chair tipped to one side but then it settled down again.

"I'm sorry," said the woman. "I wish we could stay near, but it looks like we're going to drift apart."

Rafe, too, could see they were moving farther from one another. "I wish we could too," he said, feeling as if he were saying goodbye to someone he'd known a long time rather than just a few minutes. "Would you do me a favor?"

"What is it?"

"Would you play something on your cello?"

"I haven't played for anyone since all this happened. Who knows when I'll have an audience again?"

She stepped over to pick up the cello and the bow. Then she sat back down on the crate. "Have you ever heard a cello before?" she asked.

"Maybe? I'm not sure."

"I will play Cello Suite No. 1 by Johann Sebastian Bach. It's the greatest work ever written for the instrument."

She raised her bow and put her other hand around the neck. And then she started to play. The music was low and rhythmic and solemn and beautiful. Holding Buddy in his arms, Rafe stood at the window and listened. The music filled his heart. He listened as the barrels floated in the other direction, listened as the woman grew smaller and the music fainter, listened until once more he could hear only the sound of water lapping against his room.

5

Serpent

In the morning, Rafe woke to the sound of rain. It wasn't the sound that he was used to, the distant tapping on the roof of the house. This louder barrage of sound was directly overhead, on the flat roof that was the other side of his ceiling and all that separated him from the elements.

The air was chilly, and Buddy had buried himself under the covers except for the very tip of his nose. "Come on, boy, time to wake up." Even though Rafe didn't have to get up for school, or join his parents at the breakfast table, he still thought that he ought to get up, get dressed, and pretend that there was some order and purpose to the day. He rose and changed into his clothes, realizing that in another week or so he would have to figure out a way to wash them.

Even though it was raining, he still had to take Buddy up to the roof to relieve himself. He didn't have a raincoat, only an old garbage bag that his mother had given him to fill with clothes he didn't need. He punched holes in it for his head and arms and wore it like a poncho. Halfway up the ladder, his foot slipped on the wet rung and Buddy yelped as Rafe managed to land on the one below. He went even slower after that and made it safely to the top. But it was no fun standing on the roof as the wind made his room rock back and forth.

When they got back inside, Buddy shook himself madly, causing water drops to fly everywhere. "Thanks for the second soaking," Rafe said. "If you're finished, old Buddy," he said, scratching the dog between the ears, "it's time for breakfast. I guess we better have only one can. We have a pretty good supply, but we don't know how long it will have to last us. Let's see what we get."

Buddy watched with keen interest as the boy opened a can with the screwdriver and rock. "Nice one! Spaghetti and meatballs. Mom never used to let me have this."

He divided the can in two, giving Buddy an extra meatball, which clearly pleased the dog, who ate with gusto. Afterward Buddy sat on the floor licking his front teeth over and over. Rafe himself thought the meal would have tasted better warmed up. Still, he ate every last bit of it.

And then the thunder started.

It was shockingly loud, as if the sky was cracking in half. Buddy jumped into the air and landed in Rafe's lap, pushing himself under Rafe's shirt.

"That's okay, boy, it won't hurt us. At least I hope not." The two of them cowered together as lightning lit up the sky so brightly that it hurt Rafe's eyes. The thunder crashed again. Rafe had never seen or heard anything like it. Was there something different about the storm, the way there was something different about the world? Meanwhile, the lightning turned everything white, and the thunder made him cover his ears with his hands.

The room had been rocking steadily but now it rose. It rose, hovered, and plummeted downward, jolting them off the bed and onto the floor. The storm was turning the sea wild, turning it into a roiling roller coaster. They went up and down again and again.

Rafe managed to hold onto the whimpering Buddy and climb back onto the bed. When he looked up at the window (thank goodness it was closed), he could see a wave growing larger and larger. It slammed into the room, turning it right around. But somehow, they remained afloat.

"We just have to ride it out, Buddy," said Rafe, trying to sound brave even if he didn't feel it. They stayed on the bed as it slid across the floor, banging into the desk chair and the laundry basket.

At last the storm began to subside. The thunder sounded farther away and the lightning dimmed. But the rain kept falling and the room swayed gently in the waves.

"That was a rough one," Rafe said, giving Buddy a hug. "I think we can get out of bed now. Look at this room! Everything's been knocked about. We better clean up."

As he began to put things back, Rafe realized that this was the first time he had ever cleaned up his room without being told. He didn't want to think about his mother and father, not after having just gone through the storm, so he started whistling a tune that was popular at school, or used to be. He wasn't a very good whistler, but then a lot of other kids his age couldn't whistle at all. The best whistler at school had no doubt been Allen Gilruddy. Allen could do that two-finger whistle that carried for miles and miles. He and Allen weren't really friends, although they had gone to one another's birthday parties when they were little, and once, playing pick-up baseball, Allen had been a captain and had made Rafe his third pick. Earlier this year Allen had done an oral presentation on the melting of the polar ice caps and the plight of the polar bears. But where was Allen Gilruddy now? Was he floating in his own room? Or was he gone?

Despite himself, Rafe's thoughts had taken a dark turn. Doing something practical might help, like catching some of that rain to use for drinking and washing. He emptied his bucket of Lego and held it out the window until it became almost too heavy. He hauled it back in and then filled up his water bottle, his plastic ukulele, his old set of toy teacups, anything that could hold water.

By the time he ran out of containers, the rain had turned into mist. The late sun (for the storm had taken up most of the day) could be seen just above the horizon. Probably it would be a good idea to take Buddy onto the roof for some fresh air and exercise.

He put up the ladder, and the dog, who now understood what the ladder meant, willingly jumped into his arms. They got up onto the roof. The mist made his skin feel damp, but he was glad to get out of the confines of the room. "Come on, time for a walk," he said and began marching in a rectangle around the perimeter of the roof. Buddy trotted at his heels. They went around ten, fifteen, twenty times before something made Rafe stop.

A sea serpent.

It was out there, a creature half submerged in the water, with an elongated body, a neck shaped like an *S* and a tail. Through the mist it looked like the fuzzy picture he had once seen of the Loch Ness Monster, the sea serpent that was supposed to live in a lake in Scotland. What if the rising sea had swamped the lake and freed the creature to roam through the ocean? He could see that it was angling toward them, getting closer. Was it curious? Was it dangerous? Did it eat humans and dogs and whatever else it could find? Had he and Buddy survived only to end up as serpent chow?

If only he had a weapon, something to defend them with. Not that he wanted to kill anything, but it might be a matter of survival. And while these thoughts were going through his mind, the serpent got closer and closer, and the mist melted away so that he could see what it actually was.

It was garbage.

Maybe debris was a better word. The body of the serpent was, in fact, a long wooden deck with a bunch of junk piled on top of it, bits of metal, hubcaps, broken furniture. The swan-like neck was a streetlight. And as it came alongside, he could see that the tail was made from a twisted rain gutter.

Now that he saw it clearly, he was almost embarrassed to have mistaken it for a living creature. But perhaps under the circumstances it wasn't surprising that his imagination had gotten away from him.

And then Rafe realized something. Something that froze his heart.

The serpent wasn't alive. Nothing was. Other than the cellist, he hadn't seen a single living thing. Not anywhere. He hadn't seen a seagull in the sky, nor a dolphin, minnow or crab in the water. He hadn't heard a bee buzz or been bitten by a mosquito or annoyed by a fly.

Where were all the animals? Were they gone too?

Rafe picked up Buddy and hugged him tight. He hugged him so long that the dog finally squirmed out of his arms.

"Come on, boy," he said finally. "Let's go back in."

6

50 R.D.

A few days later Rafe spotted a small wooden crate floating by. He didn't know what was inside it, but almost anything could be a help, so he leaped into action.

He tried to use the lacrosse stick but the crate was too large. All he managed to do was turn it onto its side. But the crate had a rope handle on the end. He just needed something that could hook onto it. The end of the ladder was a possibility, but he couldn't risk dropping or otherwise damaging it.

Rafe hurried to the closet and began pulling things out. He found a bungee cord that he sometimes used for holding stuff on his bike rack. It did have a little metal hook on each end but the bungee part was like a giant elastic band rather than a rope. It was worth a try.

Back to the window he went. The crate had floated a little farther away, but he tossed out the end of the cord and hooked the rope handle on the first try. Hauling something in with a bungee cord turned out to be harder than he had expected. Every time he pulled, the cord just stretched farther and the crate stayed put in the water. Then the hook got loose of the handle and the elastic cord whipped back toward Rafe, just missing his eye.

He tried again. Slow and easy. He pulled and pulled and at last the crate began to move through the water toward the room. He used one hand over the other and the crate bumped the wall and then began to rise. When it was in the air, it started to bounce up and down so Rafe stopped until it became still. Even slower this time he pulled it upward. It must have taken him an hour of painful effort to get the crate close enough for him to grab onto the rope handle.

He had expected the crate to be heavy, but it turned out to be rather light. He carried it to the middle of the room and put it down on the floor.

The dog watched him, his head tilted in curiosity. "What do you think's inside it, Buddy? I really hope it's food. How about bags of potato chips? No, something more filling. Beef jerky! You'd like that, too, wouldn't you, boy? Or else a raincoat and rubber boots—that would be useful. Or batteries for my flashlight. What does it say on the side of the crate? *50 R.D.* I have no idea what that means. Well, let's find out. I just have to find something to pry it open with."

A pen wouldn't work. Nor would nail clippers. But then Rafe remembered the screwdriver that he used to open the cans. "One of the most useful inventions known to humans— and dogs," he said as he pushed the tip under the lid of the crate and began to pry it up. "Hold on, Buddy. We're about to learn what *50 R.D.* means." He shifted the screwdriver along the edge and pried some more, shifted it again, until at last he could yank off the top.

He and Buddy both stared into the crate.

"Rubber ducks? Fifty *rubber ducks*? Those stupid things that kids like to play with in the bathtub? Aw, Buddy, this is like opening the worst birthday present of your entire life."

He tried and failed to see anything funny about it. He was too disappointed. And for at least two hours, he tried to think of a use for them. But he couldn't, not a single thing. Buddy wasn't even interested in chewing on one.

Finally, he thought of something. Not useful, but something. He took a spool of strong button thread from his desk drawer and tied one of the rubber ducks around the neck. Then he tied a second and third, until all fifty were strung on the line. He picked them up, went over to the window as Buddy watched, and keeping hold of the end of the thread, he tossed them out.

The rubber ducks bobbed up and down, turning themselves upright. At first, they were in a jumble, but after a while, the movement of the room caused the line to straighten out. He pressed a thumbtack from his bulletin board into the wooden windowsill and tied the end of the thread around it.

The fifty rubber ducks bobbed along in their row, following the room as it drifted on the sea.

"Totally pointless," Rafe said as he watched them.

7

Conversations with a Rabbit

Back in the old days (that is, the days before he found himself floating on the sea), Rafe had been burdened by homework. There was always too much of it, in his opinion, and some of it was really hard. He had come home from what turned out to be his last day of school with four pages of math questions, a French conversation and a book report on a novel that he hadn't even started reading.

The truth was that he'd always hated doing homework, not when he could play a video game or watch a movie or ride his bike with Ravi from next door. (Don't think about Ravi, Rafe told himself.) His report cards often said that he didn't live up to his potential, and when his mom and dad would point this out, he'd say, "But that just means I'm smarter than my marks show. Isn't that good?"

So Rafe found it extremely strange that he began to miss doing homework. In fact, he missed it so much that he decided to do the work he had. Well, maybe not the math questions, but he wrote out a conversation in French that he liked so much he spoke it out loud several times.

"Où est-que tu habite, Rafe?"

"Moi, je reste sur la mer."

"Tu as un bateau de maison?"

"Non, j'habite dans un bateau de chambre!"

The book report was going to take more time because Rafe had been labeled by the school a "reluctant reader," and the book, *Conversations with a Rabbit*, wasn't a comic book but a novel. On the cover it said that the book had been runner-up for the Dunkelman Prize and the Kloz-Breslin Medal and the Purple Flamingo Award, all of which meant that it was only second best. But with so much time on his hands, Rafe decided to lounge on his bed and start reading.

The story was about a girl (he didn't usually read stories about girls) whose parents were having an argument. They were arguing about where to move. The dad wanted to move to Portland, Oregon, and the mother wanted to move to some islands called the Azores. There was no reason given for why they had to move anywhere, only that the girl didn't want to go.

Tired of hearing her parents argue, she went into the backyard and sat at their picnic bench. After a while she noticed something moving in the grass. It was a rabbit. The girl froze. The rabbit kept eating, munching grass with little motions of its teeth and then looking up again and listening with its upright ears. It was a pretty good size, speckled brown, with a bit of white around its eyes and under its mouth, which was turned down a little as if in a pout. The girl thought it was adorable, especially the way it moved forward on its small front paws and powerful back legs, a sort of half walk, half hop.

The girl kept quiet, at least until she accidentally banged her knee on the picnic table and said "Ouch!" The rabbit stood up on its hind legs, sniffing the air and looking about with its big dark eyes as its ears swiveled one way and another.

"Who's that?" said the rabbit.

"I'm sorry?" said the girl.

The rabbit looked at her. "There you are," it said. "I'm rather far-sighted, you know. I can't see things close up so well. You aren't planning to shoot me, are you?"

"No," the girl managed to say. "No, never."

"Good," said the rabbit, and it put its head down and continued to eat. The girl watched in amazement. A rabbit talking to a girl? How was it possible? But right now she felt so strongly the need of a friend that she didn't care whether it was human or not.

The girl sighed loudly.

The rabbit looked up. "Oh dear," it said. "That doesn't sound good."

"No, it's not."

The animal sat on its haunches. "Go on, then. Let's hear it. I'm a good listener, you know. It's the big ears."

For the next few days when Rafe wasn't taking Buddy for a walk on the roof or opening cans, or holding out the bucket during a brief rain to collect fresh water or washing his clothes, he was lying on his bed reading. The rabbit really was a good listener, and every day the girl would come out for a long talk about being a kid without having any say in what happens to her.

In the first chapters the book was kind of slow, but Rafe wasn't bored. And then some things happened in the story that got a bit more exciting. Looking for some tender shoots to eat, the rabbit ventured into the backyard of the girl's neighbor, an old and grouchy man who was always complaining that the girl made too much noise or left her bike on the sidewalk, or just about anything else. The girl looked out her bedroom window and saw the rabbit in the neighbor's backyard and immediately grew afraid. She was about to go down to warn the rabbit when she saw the grouchy old man come out his own back door. He was carrying a net on a long pole, the sort of net a person would use to scoop up a fish caught on a hook. (Rafe couldn't help thinking it would have been a pretty useful thing for *him* to have.) The old man crept forward toward the rabbit, who was enjoying some new lettuce leaves in the grouch's garden.

Out her room and down the stairs the girl ran. She threw open the back door and burst into the yard, but it was too late. The man had already slammed down his net.

"Got ya!" the man cried. "Thought you could eat my lettuce, you little pest? Well, you'll go nicely in an old-fashioned stew, the kind my grandma used to make."

The girl began to plead with the man to let the rabbit go. It was such a nice, thoughtful rabbit, she said. It was her friend. But the man just said, "I always thought you were a strange girl, but now you sound like you're off your rocker." He took the struggling rabbit ("Help, help!" it was crying, but apparently the man couldn't understand it) into his garage and shut the door behind him.

At this point Rafe had to close the book and stand up. His heart was beating fast and he couldn't read any more. It seemed strange to care so much about a rabbit, but maybe that was because he was without television. He was hungry for stories as much as food.

Rafe picked up Buddy and gave him a kiss on the snout, then went to the window to look out at the wide water. There were little, gentle waves moving the room along, but moving it to where? Was there land somewhere in the distance? Or was there only water, water and nothing else? And as he was wondering he saw something floating nearby.

8

The Age of Sail

It was a flat, square package, riding gently on the waves toward the room. Rafe had no idea what it was, but after the incident of the crate filled with rubber ducks, he certainly wasn't going to get excited. Still, he got his lacrosse stick and waited patiently until the package was bumping right up against the room. With the stick, he pushed it flat against the wall and then, using all the pressure he could manage, lifted up the stick. Trapped between the stick and the wall, the package inched upward. When it was high enough, Rafe reached down with one hand and got a hold of it.

The package said right on it what was inside. *Four-Person Tent! Great for camping or backyard fun! Water resistant! Easy to put up!*

Even though he had tried not to get his hopes up, Rafe couldn't help feeling disappointed yet again. A tent without any ground to put it on was about as useful as a crate of rubber ducks. Besides, the tent was missing the second package containing the tent poles.

And then it hit him.

The Age of Sail.

The Age of Sail was a documentary that he had once watched with his parents on television. His parents had loved documentaries. He remembered this one was about the eighteenth century, or was it the seventeenth? Anyway, it was about the time when countries like Spain and Portugal and the Netherlands and England had mighty ships that traversed the oceans by using only the power of wind. They used these ships to explore the continents and bring back spices and even do battle.

A sail. He could make a sail out of the tent!

If Rafe could fix up a sail, he could get the room to move much faster and farther. He might discover land, or an island at least. He might find more food or other people. And he would be *doing* something rather than nothing.

The only problem was that the tent wasn't really shaped like a sail but more like a giant bowl. (The illustration on the package showed that the tent was round.) Also, a sail needed a stiff mast to hang on and he couldn't see any way to get a mast or, even if he found something that might work, to attach it to the room so that it stood up. But then he remembered seeing a YouTube video of a person on a surfboard, holding onto a parachute. The parachute filled with wind and pulled him swiftly along the water. It seemed to Rafe that the tent was actually more like a parachute than a sail. It just might work.

Leaving behind an offended Buddy, he took the package up to the roof and ripped it open. The tent was made of pretty strong material, and there were even cords sewn all along the bottom. All he had to do was gather up the cords and attach them to the end of the room. Then the tent would hang down over the side until the wind filled it up. The question was, how to attach the cords? He thought of a dozen different and complicated ways before coming up with a simpler idea. A nail. If he could hammer a nail into the top of the roof, he could tie the cords to it.

First of all, he needed to find the nail. Back in his room he looked around. He couldn't see any nails at all, at least none that were big enough. There were nails holding together his bookshelves, but even if he could smash a shelf and get one out, it would be too small. Then he looked at his bulletin board. He knew that it was hung on something so he took it down and, yes, there was a nail in the wall. In fact, it was far bigger than it needed to be to hold up the bulletin board. And it wasn't very secure, because his father (who hadn't been very handy with tools) had simply banged it into the plaster. Rafe put his hand on the nail and tugged. It came out easily.

Back up to the roof he went, this time taking the nail and also the rock that he used to help open cans. He paced one end of the roof to find the center point and then held the nail carefully and banged. He was lucky, for there must have been a wooden stud underneath the plaster. Bit by bit the nail went in. And when it was halfway, he stopped and pulled at it. The nail held firm.

Next he lay the tent out on the roof and tied the cords to the nail. So far so good. Now all he had to do was push the tent over the edge of the roof so that it hung there until the wind picked up.

Over the edge it went. But there was no wind and the tent hung down past the end of the room like a deflated balloon. So he went back down, and while he scratched Buddy on the stomach, he read three chapters of *Conversations with a Rabbit*. In the book the girl couldn't think about anything besides what was going to happen to the rabbit. So she waited until the late afternoon, when the grouchy old man always took his nap (she wasn't allowed to make noise outside), and put a crate up against the man's garage wall so that she could see through the open window. There was the rabbit, just sitting in the cage.

"Hi!" she whispered.

"Oh, it's you. How nice to see a friendly face."

"Can you get out of the cage?"

"I don't mean to sound sarcastic, but if I could have, I would have. The latch is on the outside. I can't reach it from here. So it goes."

"What do you mean, 'So it goes'?"

"Oh, it's just an expression we rabbits use. It means that there is nothing you can do about it. A farmer sets a trap and catches your mother. A hunter waits behind a log and shoots your brother. An eagle swoops down and takes your little one from the nest. The life of a rabbit is full of terrible things. Rabbits are very resigned to whatever happens. Really, we have no choice. When you are a rabbit, death is always a possibility."

"Well, I just don't think that's right," said the girl. "I don't think you should be resigned. Why does that grouchy old man get to decide what happens to you? Just because you ate some of his lettuce?"

"You sound just like my cousin. He was always railing at fate. 'It isn't fair, what happens to us,' he would say. 'Rabbits shouldn't just take it. Rabbits should rule the world.' And then he got eaten by a fox."

"I still think your cousin was right. And I'm going to do something about it. You're my friend. I'm not just going to let this happen to you. All I have to do is climb through the window and let you out."

"It's a very long drop on the other side. I don't advise it."

"Here I come," said the girl.

Rafe looked up from the book. Had the room moved? No, it was his imagination. The girl in the book was doing the same thing that he was doing with the parachute. He was also taking fate in his own hands—

It *did* move! He definitely felt it that time. "Hey, Buddy!" he said to the dog, who was looking a little concerned. "The wind is picking up. That was the tent pulling us. I want to go see."

He went to the window and put up the ladder. Buddy started yipping with excitement, but again Rafe decided it best to leave him behind. He climbed up and onto the roof. All was still. The ropes of the tent were still tied to the nail, disappearing over the edge. But then he felt air on his back and a moment later there was a flapping sound and the tent rose up past the edge of the roof. It was only half-filled with air, but it really did look like a parachute. It dipped down, then up and then the wind blew stronger, and the tent rose and filled out to its full shape. Sure enough the room began to move through the water.

But Rafe could see right away that there was a problem. The room didn't have a pointed end like the front of a boat that would allow it to cut straight through the water. Instead, it had a flat end that battered and bumped against the waves. Sometimes the water struck more on the left, sometimes on the right, so that as the parachute pulled it forward the room moved in a series of jerks and stutters, first one way and then another. The wind picked up even more and the room actually tipped forward, the back end rising up out of the water and then smacking down again.

Clearly Rafe hadn't thought his idea through. The room might tip over or get pulled under or even break apart. He was trying to think what was the best thing to do now when a huge gust filled the tent so that it ballooned outward and propelled the room forward with such thrust that Rafe's feet went out from under him.

He fell—*thump!*—onto his back. It hurt, but that wasn't the worst of it. The worst was that the room was moving all over the place—jerking left, jerking right, plunging down and up again. It was moving so much that Rafe couldn't get back onto his feet.

Even as the room was rising and plunging, Rafe saw something. He saw another person. A man. He was floating on a sign that must have been five feet high. Grand Luxor Hotel. The man was sitting on top of the sign and he was waving and shouting at Rafe. But Rafe didn't have a chance to shout back before the room shot past.

Somehow he had to stop the room. If he didn't, it was going to crack like an egg and he and Buddy would plunge into the water and drown. How far had the parachute pulled the room? Probably as much as he usually travelled in several days, but still there was no land in sight. Using the tent as a sail had been rash. Maybe the girl in *Conversations with a Rabbit* was right in believing that you shouldn't just accept your fate, but that didn't mean you were always smart about it.

He knew what he had to do. He had to take charge of his fate again, but this time by stopping what he had started.

Since the room was bouncing around too much for him to stand up, he began to crawl. One hand and then another, he moved slowly forward. It seemed to take forever but at last he got within reach of the nail.

He put his hand into his pocket and felt the handle of the screwdriver. The end was sharp—every couple of days he would rub it against the rock so that it would pierce cans. Now he needed it to act as a knife. It was a bit awkward to hold for a cutting movement but he managed to begin sawing through one of the cords. It wasn't thick and only took five or six strokes before snapping. There were seven more and he started on the next.

He cut all the cords on one side, which turned out to be another mistake because it caused only that side of the tent to collapse. The other side was still full of air and the room got dragged to the left, tilting dangerously over. Faster he cut, until there was just one cord left. The pull of the wind caused it to snap on its own and the tent fell into the sea. Suddenly free, the room rocked violently up and down, turning in a circle.

Rafe could hear Buddy barking hysterically. "Don't worry, Buddy," he called as the room began to settle down, "we're okay now."

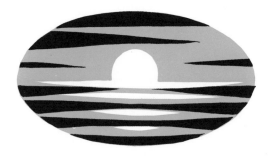

9

Family Resemblance

Well, that had been a terrible plan. He had almost wrecked his room, had terrified his dog and had managed to see no land at all.

And yet as he thought about it more, Rafe realized that one good thing had come out of being dragged furiously around by the wind. He'd seen another person. The man floating on a sign. True, he had gone by so fast that they hadn't had time to say a single word to one another, but even just seeing another person made him feel a little less alone. And the fact that he had now seen two people (including the woman with the cello) meant that there must be other floaters out there.

Even his relationship with the cello player hadn't lasted very long. But he could still hear in his mind the beautiful music she had played for him. Encountering other people wasn't just pleasant or interesting. It was crucial to his survival. Without seeing other human beings, he would surely be plunged into despair.

The question was, what could he do to improve his chances of having more encounters?

Rafe had seen the man on the sign because—well, because the sign was so big and noticeable. But what about his own room? The outside walls were a whitish-gray color. They didn't look like much of anything at all, and from even a short distance, he bet that his room blended into the background of water and sky. What he needed to do was make his room more visible so that other people could see it. Yes, that was it! He had to decorate the outside walls.

The only problem was that he had nothing to decorate them with. But maybe he would get lucky and find something bobbing in the ocean. When Rafe found the tent, he had figured out what he might do with it. This time he knew what he wanted but he had to hope that it came by.

For the next three days, Rafe spent all of his free time standing at the window with his lacrosse stick in hand. He couldn't watch and read at the same time, so he occupied himself by singing. Strangely, he couldn't remember any of the hit songs that all the kids had liked. Instead, he could only recall the songs from when he was little. So he sang "Row, Row, Row Your Boat" and "This Land Is Your Land." He sang a funny song that his dad used to belt out, "Yes, We Have No Bananas." And when he ran out of songs, he made up his own.

It's so very, very nice
So I'll stop and say it twice.
It's so very, very nice upon the sea.

But it's very, very sad
To be the only lad.
Yes, it's very, very sad upon the sea.

And it's very, very dull

Without whale or crab or gull.

Yes, it's very, very dull upon the sea.

And it's really quite a question

To have no comprehension.

Yes, it's really quite a question on the sea.

And it makes one quite a nerd

To sing a song that can't be heard.

Yes, it makes one quite a nerd upon the sea.

As he sang, Rafe managed to scoop up three dozen more cans, including ten flat tins of sardines. He didn't love sardines, but he knew they were full of protein and that sardine oil was good for him and Buddy too. He also caught a large bottle of lemon juice that was three-quarters full. Rafe had once read that sailors on long voyages who didn't have enough fruit and vegetables drank a little lemon juice to fend off scurvy. He started to take a tablespoon a day. It had a nice, tart taste.

He also scooped up a rubber ball (a good toy for Buddy),
a television remote control and a Tupperware container of
old family photographs.

He got sidetracked for a full day by the photographs. Most
were in black-and-white. A man and woman standing in front
of a big car. Two teenage boys in bathing suits lying on beach
towels and smiling. A birthday party with little kids in paper
hats. A portrait of a woman in a wedding gown with puffy
sleeves. But there were color photographs too. A girl playing with a dog in a backyard (he showed that one to Buddy).

A high school basketball game. A trip to the zoo. Studying them, he could follow kids as they grew up and adults as they grew old. He saw people who resembled each other and must have been brothers and sisters or cousins. The people in the photos weren't his family, but they were *a* family. He spent a long time with them before placing the photographs back in the container and putting it under his bed.

And then he went back to the window. And miracle of miracles, he caught a can of paint.

It wasn't a big can, but it was enough to make some difference. It was purple, a color that Rafe had never liked. But as long as it was dark enough, he couldn't have cared less.

He didn't catch the can until late in the afternoon, when the sun was already going down, but he didn't want to wait another day in case he missed some other floater. Nor, despite the episode with the tent, did he stop and think again about whether his plan had any flaws. He knew that he ought to, but he had to do something. So he got out the ladder, hooked it onto the roof, and then standing halfway he used a homemade brush made from a Nerfball tied to the end of a Harry Potter wand. In large letters he painted:

RAFE SAYS HI

He could only paint that way on the wall with the window. So he climbed onto the roof, lay flat on his stomach, and painted the same words near the top of the other walls. He had to paint them upside down and backward, which wasn't easy. And since he had some paint left, he painted on the roof for good measure.

Exhausted, he went back inside, opened two cans for dinner (pickled mushrooms and cream of asparagus soup) and then collapsed onto his bed. Buddy lay down beside him, a spot of purple on his nose.

10

Dao

Rafe thought that the walls could use even more painting, and he spent a couple of days fishing, but all he caught was a soggy DVD box set of *Happy Days*, Season 5, and a headless doll.

He didn't see any floaters, either.

"Hey, Buddy," he said the next morning. "I think it's Saturday. At least I think I think it might be Saturday. Shall we go to the farmers' market? Or maybe to the mall? How about a run in the ravine? Oh, wait. There are no Saturdays anymore. No Mondays or Tuesdays or Fridays, either. There are just days, Buddy, endless holidays. Isn't that great?"

There was absolutely nothing to do. They went up to the roof for a walk in the morning and then again after lunch. Then he remembered that he hadn't picked up *Conversations with a Rabbit* for several days. So he sat back on his bed and ruffled Buddy's ears and read how the girl, ignoring the rabbit's warnings, wiggled through the garage window and tumbled down without hurting herself too much. Then she went to the cage, undid the latch and picked the large rabbit up with both hands.

The rabbit had never been picked up before and protested about feeling "undignified," but the girl just told him to shush and went to the garage door, pulled it up and got them outside. She was just about to set him down on the grass when she heard "Hey, you! Stop thief!" The grouchy old man had spotted them. So she started to run, holding the confused rabbit like a football under her arm.

She got to her own front lawn where her bicycle was leaning against a tree. She dropped the rabbit into the front basket ("Oopf! That hurts!"), jumped on the bike and took off.

Fast as she could she pedaled down the street, turning her head to see the man shaking his fist at her.

"Where are we going?" asked the frightened rabbit.

"You and I," said the girl, "are going on a great adventure."

"Rabbits don't like adventures."

"They don't talk either," said the girl. "You're a different sort of rabbit."

"Perhaps," said the rabbit, "it's more a case of your being a different sort of girl. And by the way, you're going awfully fast."

Rafe stopped at the end of the chapter. He would have liked to continue reading but didn't want to get to the end too quickly. So he went over to his desk. "You know that you're really desperate when you decide to do your math homework," he said, but for the next hour he was grateful for having something to occupy his mind.

When he was done, he continued to sit at his desk. For no particular reason he said aloud:

"Rafe says hi."

He shouted it. *"Rafe says hi!"*

Buddy looked at him.

And again, *"RAFE SAYS HI!"*

When he stopped, the room seemed even quieter than usual. And then he heard something. A voice.

"Hi.

"Hi!

"Hi, hi, hi!"

"Huh?" Rafe said. He turned in his chair and looked out the window, but from his desk he couldn't see anything. Had he imagined it? No, for Buddy had gotten up and was standing under the window, his nose lifted and his tail wagging.

Rafe jumped over to the window and looked all around. But he didn't see anything—not until he looked straight down.

And saw a girl. A very young girl, six or seven years old. She looked small for her age, with a round face and big eyes and dark hair with straight bangs that were now growing too long so that she had to look through the strands.

She also looked thin and exhausted and scared.

Still, she managed to smile at him.

The girl was floating on a small air mattress. It had images of flamingos on it and was no doubt meant for a swimming pool. She was holding a cat. A big orange tabby that stared up at Rafe in a decidedly unfriendly way. How had they survived on a little air mattress?

"Hi, hi, hi!" the girl said again, holding up the cat as if it was the one who needed rescuing.

"You better come inside," Rafe said. "Only I don't know about that cat. You see, I have a dog."

The girl swayed back and forth as if she might faint. But she began talking. Unfortunately, it was in a language that Rafe didn't understand or even recognize. He hurried now, conking himself with the ladder even as he slid it through the window. He hooked the ladder on the sill. "Can you climb up?" He made a climbing motion with his hands.

The girl nodded and began to paddle with one hand, moving the air mattress closer. She grabbed the lowest rung of the ladder and started to pull herself up. She was weak but determined, and she somehow held onto the mewling cat while holding a string tied to the air mattress.

Up she came until she reached the window. Buddy was panting as he looked up, eager to greet a new human being. But then he saw the cat, and the cat saw him.

The cat hissed.

Buddy growled.

The cat huffed itself up to look larger and then leaped out of the girl's arms and straight toward Buddy. The dog turned and ran. The cat swiped at him with claws extended, making Buddy yelp as he scrambled under the bed. The cat hunched down and stared but didn't follow.

"Some pet you've got there," Rafe said, even though he knew she couldn't understand him. The girl didn't have the energy to jump but slowly crawled through the window until she could collapse into the room, yanking the wet air mattress after her. She looked around, her eyes growing wide, as if she had just entered the most glorious mansion. Slowly she got up and began to walk about the room. She looked at a baseball glove, switched the lamp on and off (it had no effect), picked up the copy of *Conversations with a Rabbit* and looked at the cover.

"I'm Rafe," he said, pointing to himself. "Rafe."

"*Rrrave?*"

"That's right. And you?" He pointed to her.

The girl smiled. "Dao."

"Dao," he repeated. "*Da-ow.* Is that right?"

But the girl didn't answer. Instead, she dropped to the floor, crawled under the bed and dragged out Buddy. The dog wasn't too pleased, but then he turned his head and licked every inch of the girl's face, making her giggle. The girl began scolding the cat in her language, warning it to behave. Then she put Buddy down.

Buddy was so nervous that his legs trembled. The cat merely trotted to the other side of the room and began to clean itself.

"Hi!" said the girl. She closed her eyes. "Hi, Rafe."

"Hi, ah, Dao. Are you asleep?"

She opened her eyes halfway. She pointed to her mouth.

"You're hungry? Of course, you must be starving. We can have dinner."

From under the desk, he drew out two cans and a tin of sardines, one more than usual. When the girl saw them, her eyes grew even wider.

Rafe opened them up. Besides the sardines, there were corn niblets and some sort of beef stew. Needing two more plates, he scrounged around and came up with a Frisbee for the girl and the back of a toy dump truck for the cat. He divided up the food and put the animals' dishes on the ground. The cat and the dog looked warily at each other but they began to eat.

Rafe handed the Frisbee to the girl. He broke the plastic ruler in half so they would both have something to eat with.

"Mmmm," said the girl, her mouth full. "Mmmmm."

She was almost finished before she fell asleep.

11

Gooood

Where did she come from? Wherever it was, the same catastrophe had happened there. How had she managed to survive? What had she eaten?

She slept on, her head leaning on his desk. The sun was going down. She couldn't just stay like that. She needed a bed. His room hadn't been terribly big before, but now suddenly it seemed a lot smaller. It was a good thing that Dao wasn't very big. And that she had dragged in her air mattress.

It was still damp so he dried it with some clothes and laid it down in the opposite corner from his bed. He tucked one of his sheets around it and gave up a blanket and a pillow. Gently he roused her and moved her over. He gave her one of his T-shirts and she fumbled under the covers to change. She said something he couldn't understand, closed her eyes and was asleep again.

As for the cat, she (Rafe was pretty sure the cat was female) stared at Buddy for a long time, making the dog nervous. He wouldn't settle down on the foot of Rafe's bed. Finally the cat got up, stretched and, with one quick pounce, squeezed herself between two shelves over the desk. It didn't look very comfortable, but the cat seemed to like it there. She, too, closed her eyes.

All was peaceful. That is, until Rafe woke up to the sound of Dao making noises. Awful, guttural noises. She was clearly having a nightmare. Rafe got up and sat on the floor by her bed. He took her hand. She quieted down. He looked around and noticed the headless doll that he had fished out of the sea. Gently he tucked it against Dao. She pulled it closer and grew still.

In the morning, Dao seemed to have no memory of the nightmare. She was cheerful and smiling as she got out of bed. It was almost as if she was too happy. Didn't she understand they were floating in an endless sea, that the world they had known had disappeared? But of course she was perfectly aware of it, Rafe thought. She'd been on a toy raft in a stormy sea. Yet still she was able to take pleasure in her cat, in Buddy, in the room and in him.

She was smart, a much quicker learner of languages than he was. Before the morning was out, she knew the words "Buddy," "roof," "eat," "good" and "go pee," although she said them all in her own accent. Although Rafe had desperately wanted company, he hadn't quite expected to get a roommate. Now he had to worry not only just about himself, but also about a young person. Not having any brothers or sisters, he wasn't used to having another kid around all the time.

Also, he was used to making all the decisions. Dao turned out not to be the sort of kid who just went along with everything. At dinnertime, Rafe brought out three cans. Immediately Dao reached down into the stack and took out a fourth.

"No, Dao, we have to be careful to save our food," he said. He put the can back.

She took it out again.

He put it back.

Out.

Back.

Out.

Back.

"Good," Dao said. "*Gooood.*"

"All right, fine." He grudgingly opened the four cans. He would just have to make sure they spent enough time fishing for more. Over the next few days, Dao proved stubborn about a lot of other things too. Like making her bed. And helping to wash the dishes. And brushing her teeth with the extra toothbrush that Rafe's dentist had given him. All these little arguments were tiring, and Rafe didn't know how to be stern without sounding mean. Once, he raised his voice at her because she was teasing Buddy by not giving the dog his ball. Dao got so mad that she screamed at him in her own language and then refused to say a word for the rest of the day. He almost longed for the peace of solitary living.

One afternoon Rafe lay on his bed with his hands behind his head, staring up at the ceiling. He was trying to remember as many of his birthday parties as he could. This was something new for him, thinking about life in the old days. At first he'd found it unbearable even to try.

"Hey, Dao," he said, leaning on one elbow. "Did you have birthday parties too?"

"*Pardees*," Dao said, continuing to take every last thing out of Rafe's closet in order to examine it closely.

"Please be careful with that model airplane; it took me weeks to make. What about your parents? Did you have a mom and dad?"

"*Moom* and *dood*," she said, spinning the airplane's propeller.

"I really wish I could find out who you are. What country are you from? What's your favorite food?"

"Eat?"

"No, not yet."

"Oh, oh," Dao said, pulling one last thing out of the closet.

It was an old school atlas, the one that Rafe had borrowed from his classroom the year before. "So that's where that went," he said.

Dao came over, flipping through its pages. "Hi, hi!" she said. She turned the book toward him and pointed.

"Is that where you're from, Dao? Let me see. This is the map for Southeast Asia. And the country you're pointing to is . . . Thailand. Wow, that's amazing."

Dao closed the atlas and put it back in the closet. She shoved everything else in as well and then came back to sit beside Rafe on the bed.

"Hi, Rafe," she said.

"Hi, Dao."

"Rafe good?"

"Sorry. I'm fine. Don't worry about me."

Dao sighed heavily, as if imitating an adult. She noticed the copy of *Conversations with a Rabbit* on his bed and picked it up. "Hmm," she said.

"Do you know what that animal is?" Rafe asked.

"*Gra-dtai.*"

"'*Gra-dtai*,'" he repeated. "And we say 'rabbit.'"

"Rabbit. Good, good?"

"Kind of weird, actually. But, sure, I'd say it's good. I read a chapter before bed last night. You see, the girl has helped the rabbit to escape from the grouchy man's garage. And the rabbit is like, 'What? You mean you don't have to just accept your fate?' He realizes that the girl has something to teach him too. But now they have taken off on the girl's bicycle with no idea where to go. They ride out of town and pass a bunch of farms and then they see this house standing all by itself . . ."

"Uh, uh, uh," she said, waving her hand in the air. He thought she was trying to say that he was talking too fast.

"Sorry about that. Would you like me to read you some? You won't understand it, but you might learn some new words." He pointed to the book.

She nodded. "Yes, yes, yes, yes."

He tried to start reading from where he left off, but she pulled the book from his hands, turned to the first page and made him start again. In school, Rafe had always dreaded being asked to read aloud. He was slow and he often stumbled. Once he got stuck on a word and a girl in class even laughed. But he opened the book to the first page. He tripped over a couple of words at the start but then began to read more smoothly. Dao didn't laugh or criticize him or make him repeat anything. She just listened intensely, her chin resting on her hands. It didn't seem to matter that she didn't understand, but he tried to read dramatically and use different voices for the girl and the rabbit. Rafe began to enjoy reading aloud, and when he glanced up, he saw that Dao had a dreamy look in her eyes. He read for almost an hour and then they had dinner (pumpkin pie filling, chicken noodle soup, coconut milk, some kind of spongey meat) and cleaned up, Dao helping without being asked. They went onto the roof to pee, their backs turned to one another, and then brushed their teeth and got into their beds.

Dao said something in her language.

"What's that?" he yawned.

"Rabbit?"

"Oh. Like a bedtime reading. Okay, just a few pages."

He got out of bed and came over to sit cross-legged on the floor beside her. The cat was already up on her shelf, and Buddy was on the end of Rafe's bed, but the two animals

watched them. He began to read quietly, watching Dao as
her eyes started to close.

"Rabbit good," she said.

"I think so too."

"Girl good."

"Hey, that's a new word for you."

Without opening her eyes, she moved her finger slowly in
an arc.

"Does that mean tomorrow? Sure, we can read again."

"Gooood."

Then she was asleep. Rafe leaned over and pulled up her blanket. Of course, there was nobody to put him to bed, so he did it himself.

12

Stovepipe Hat

Something woke Rafe up.

He didn't bother to keep the blind closed anymore, and the morning light caused him to blink as he listened to the sound of birds.

Birds?

Were there really birds outside? They would be the first wild animals he had seen. That would be amazing! He sat up quickly and saw that Dao was already standing beside her air mattress, wide awake.

"Birds, Dao! I hear birds!"

Both the dog and cat heard the sounds too. They were staring at the window, but the cat had its back arched up, its fur bristling. Rafe went over to the window. He didn't see birds.

He saw teenagers.

There were five of them, standing on a peaked orange roof that looked like it had once belonged to a fast-food restaurant. There were three boys and two girls wearing crazily mismatched clothes—an army jacket over a skirt, overalls with a bow tie. Each had a hat pulled down low or a scarf tied round the head. Each held a broken hockey stick or the base of a lamp or a cricket bat. These teenagers were the ones making the bird calls, and they were doing it now, trills and whistles and little pip-pip-pips with their fingers in their mouths. But seeing Rafe and Dao looking out, they stopped.

"Hi, hi, hi!" said Dao.

"Well, who have we here?" said the boy standing nearest to them on the roof. He was skinny and tall and wore a black

stovepipe hat, quite bashed in. In one hand was an iron fire-
place poker.

"I'm Rafe," said Rafe. "And this is Dao. You're the first
people we've seen in a long time. And the first who aren't
adults."

"Is that so. You hear that? We're the first!"

The others made hooting sounds and slapped each other's palms. That seemed kind of weird. Rafe noticed a girl
near the back using a paddle to maneuver the roof closer.
He said, "Did you spot us because of the purple paint on
the walls?"

"No," said the boy. "Would have passed right by. But then
I spotted these floating in the water." He took his other hand
from behind his back and held up . . . the string of rubber
ducks. "Really quite adorable, we all thought so. And that's
a funny shoebox of a home you've got there. What's inside?
Any food?"

"Sure, we have—*ow*!"

Dao had just kicked him in the shin! Looking innocent,
she said, "No. No food."

"You sure about that? You don't have anything sweet? Chocolate? Fudge? Maple syrup? Maybe just some canned fruit?"

Rafe looked at Dao. He turned back and said, "Are you out of food?"

"Us?" said the boy. "Nah, we aren't low, are we, guys? We have some nice storage space under this roof here and I'd say it's just about full."

Dao said, "No good."

Rafe looked at her with alarm. "She doesn't understand. Maybe you want to trade some things? We've got a lot of sardines."

The other teenagers laughed, until the tall boy gave them a look to make them stop. "We aren't too big on sharing. We prefer to hang onto what we have. You never know what may come, not in this crazy world we live in. Actually, some of us like it better now. Some of us didn't like the old world so much. Nobody to tell us what to do now, eh? If you don't mind, a couple of my mates here are going to come aboard your shoebox. Just to make sure everything is shipshape."

Dao tapped Rafe's shoulder. He leaned down and she spoke into his ear. "Bad smell," she said. "Bad, bad smell."

Those were Dao's words for anything she didn't like. She'd learned them after they'd eaten four cans of beans for dinner one night. In a louder voice she said, "We go bye-bye!"

Rafe looked at her again. It might be a good idea to trust her instincts. "You have a nice day," he said.

"Ah, but we're just getting to know you," said the tall boy. He turned to the others and ordered sharply, "Bring it up!" And then to Rafe and Dao he said, "You might be holding out on us. We'd like to see just what food you've got. And we could always use some extra clothes, mattresses and anything else. And look at that nice dog who keeps jumping up. I'm sure he'd be a swell companion. A dog would be fun to have around. We could teach him some tricks. We could see how long he can swim."

Rafe felt himself grow rigid. "Stay away from my dog."

But the boy had turned around to face his crew. "Come on, put down that plank! Let's raid!"

Plank? Raid? Suddenly Rafe knew what they were. They weren't ordinary kids. They were pirates! And they were going to steal everything that he and Dao had. Everything they needed to survive.

Two of them were bringing up a heavy wooden board. They swung it around and thunked the end down on Rafe's windowsill.

"Don't try to push that off now," said the tall boy. "That wouldn't be very friendly. It might even make us mad. I think I better do this myself. Permission to come aboard, Captain. Oh, wait. I don't need permission!"

The tall boy jumped up onto the plank with a dexterous leap. The others hooted their appreciation and he bowed low, doffing his hat. Then, holding out the iron poker for balance, he began to walk nimbly along the plank toward them. A wave rolled by, making the plank roll and dip. But the boy held out his arms until he was steady again.

"We have to do something," Rafe whispered to Dao.

Dao answered with a low growl. Another wave rolled by, higher than the last. The boy looked a little anxious but he managed to keep his footing. "Just like a ride at the carnival," he said. But now he got down on all fours and began to crawl along the plank. He was halfway there, his body suspended over the water. Behind him came a girl, who also got down on her knees and began to crawl.

Rafe put his hands on the end of the plank and pushed, but all he managed to do was shift it a little sideways. Another boy began to crawl after the girl. They were going to come aboard the room! They were going to plunder their supplies and steal Buddy!

"Hey, you," called Dao. "Bad boy. You want eat? I *give* food."

Before Rafe could say a word, Dao hurled a can through the window. It caught the boy's stovepipe hat, knocking it into the water.

"Hey, that's my favorite hat!"

"Hi, hi, hi!" Dao said. "Now head!"

Again she threw. She had a good arm—the can caught the boy on the ear.

"*Yow!* That hurts! Just you wait until I get over there. I'm going to—"

Another can smacked him in the chest. This time the boy looked more surprised than anything and it made him stop a moment. Just then a new wave, far bigger than the last, rolled by. The plank moved sideways and the boy's foot slipped off. He started to slide off the plank and a look of panic came over his face. He just managed to pull himself up again.

The other two behind him scrambled backward onto the roof. "You better come back," shouted the girl. "There's definitely a storm coming."

"Not until I show these two who's the king of the castle," the boy said, his eyes dark. "You two are going to regret—"

Rafe threw the can this time. It caught the boy square on the forehead. The boy looked dizzy for a moment and then a really big wave caused the roof to rise and the room to fall. The plank made a creaking noise and the end pulled away from the windowsill, plunging downward. The two watched the boy hold onto the plank as it hit the water. He came up sputtering, his arms flailing as he tried to keep afloat.

"Save me! Save me!"

"We better help," Rafe said. "We need to lower something down for him to grab."

But the waves were pushing the roof and the room away from one another. Someone in the boy's crew was trying to hold out a broken hockey stick to him. He reached for it just as a new wave spun the room around, causing Rafe and Dao to lose sight of him.

"Hold onto something!" Rafe shouted. The storm was breaking over them, rain pouring down and lightning flashing in the sky. What was there to hold onto? The bed began to jump as if alive. Everything on the shelves came crashing down. The animals flew across the room. Dao grabbed onto the only thing she could. She grabbed onto Rafe.

13

Riding a Giraffe

The storm lasted into the night, but by morning it was over. Rafe woke up to the sun shining in through the window and a clear blue sky. His bed was turned sideways in the room and the air mattress was pushed into a corner. Dao was still asleep with Buddy pushed up against her. When Rafe looked down at the end of the bed, he saw the cat staring at him.

Other than a bruise on Rafe's arm (he couldn't remember how he got it), everyone had come out of the storm unscathed. Dao woke up, hugged Buddy, and then they began cleaning up the room. They put back everything that had fallen from the shelves. They pushed the beds in place. They gathered up the cans that had rolled everywhere.

Days went by and turned into a week and then another week. Nothing dramatic happened—a pleasant change, in Rafe's opinion. They ate the last goodies that Rafe had forgotten were in his drawer, took their exercise up on the roof, read *Conversations with a Rabbit*, finally reaching the point that Rafe had got to so that now the story was new to him. The rabbit had no trouble finding food, nibbling the grass and wildflowers whenever they stopped. But it was trickier for the girl.

Sometimes a farm family invited her in for a meal. (She told them that she was on her way to work on her uncle's farm.) Once she got a meal at a village diner in exchange for washing dishes. On these occasions, the rabbit would wait outside for her, hiding under a hedge or in a ditch. Then they would be off again.

As they rode along, the girl asked a lot of questions. What did the rabbit think happened to a person when she died?

Was it wrong to do something bad for a good reason?

Or something good for a bad reason?

The girl never seemed to find clear answers to her questions. The rabbit's answer about death was that since most rabbits get eaten by a wolf or a fox or an eagle by the time they're one year old, they prefer to think about trying to stay alive. Sometimes she herself would think of an answer and the rabbit would respond in a way that made her change her mind. The book made Rafe want to ask some questions of his own.

Why was there water everywhere?

Could people have somehow stopped the land from disappearing?

Were humans supposed to become extinct, just like the dinosaurs had?

When they weren't reading, or fishing for cans, or exercising on the roof, Dao would ask Rafe to help her speak better. Sometimes Rafe pointed to objects in the room or pictures in his kid's encyclopedia. Or he used actions to show "running" or "angry." One morning he suggested that they have a practice conversation.

"I'll start," Rafe said. "Hello, Dao. What do you want to do today?"

"Hmm. Today I want to ride giraffe."

"Huh?"

"No, no. I mean today I want have—want *to* have—rain in my shoe."

"I don't think—"

"No, no, no! I mean today I want to sing with my belly button."

"Gee, Dao, I don't know where we went wrong."

"You think I mean it? I fool Rafe! Ha ha ha ha ha!"

"Very funny, very funny," Rafe said, half annoyed even as he laughed. "The truth is, you're an awfully fast learner. I'm trying to learn your language, but all I know so far is *saw-wat-dee*."

"Hi!" chirped Dao.

"And *la-goon*."

"You mean *la-gon*. Bye-bye!"

"And *my-pen-rye*."

"No problem!"

"But you know so much more, Dao. You use words I didn't teach you. And you seem to understand so much. How can you learn so fast?"

"Good head," Dao said, patting herself.

"That's true. But there's got to be some other reason."

"Yes. There is other reason. You want to know my secret?"

"I do."

"What do you say?"

"Please."

"In Thai?"

"Let me think. Oh, I've got it. *Garuna.*"

"Okay," she giggled. "My secret is . . . TV!"

"TV. You're serious?"

"Yes, serious. At home I watch TV. You know *Friends*? I see every one many times. Learn so much."

"Well, I guess that explains it."

"Best show ever," Dao said.

14

Noise

On another day Dao was watching for cans out the window while the cat cleaned herself, Buddy chewed on his ball, and Rafe paced back and forth. "We've got to do something, Dao," he said. "I mean, things are a lot better now that you're here. But we're still stuck in this room, in the middle of nowhere. What happens when winter comes? Or if the room springs a leak? I mean, a million things could happen."

"We be like rabbit," Dao said. "Think only nice things."

"Maybe that works for rabbits, but I don't think that will work for us. The only hope that I can see is to find some more people. Not pirates, of course, but regular people."

"People?"

"Like us. More like us."

"Good people," said Dao.

"Exactly. The question is how. We can't just wait for somebody to spot us. We have to find a way to attract more attention. The messages I painted on the outside walls aren't doing it. We have to do something more. We need people to find us."

"Make noise," Dao said with a shrug.

"Noise?"

"My family is *big*. I want Mama, Papa, I make noise. Bang! Boom! Works good."

Rafe stopped pacing. "I think you're onto something, Dao. Sound travels far over water. We have to make a whole lot of noise."

"*Woo-woo, woo-woo!*"

"Not in here. Up on the roof. And we have to be even louder. Of course, it's a risk—we could attract more pirates.

But I think we'll have to take the chance. If only we had some kind of loudspeaker. We don't have electricity or any equipment, so I guess we'll have to go back to the basics."

"Ah, the basics," said Dao. "What are basics?"

"You'll see."

Rafe got to work. He went into his closet and came out again with two bristol board posters. On one of them he had shown the life cycle of a worker bee. The other was a project on the ancient city of Pompeii. Two thousand years ago Pompeii had been destroyed by a volcano that poured lava down on it. There had been warnings—tremors and small earthquakes—but the Romans didn't know what they meant. Rafe wondered whether there had been warnings for what had happened this time. Maybe there had been signs that something was wrong with the Earth. Had the politicians or scientists not understood or, worse, did they choose to ignore the warnings?

Dao examined the projects. "Hmm, very nice."

"We're going to recycle these, Dao. We're going to turn them into simple megaphones. See, we just roll this poster up so that one end has a little opening and the other end has a big opening. I'll use the last of the tape to hold it this way. Now the other one."

Dao watched closely. When he was finished, Rafe handed her one and she put it on her head like a pointed hat.

"Is that another joke?"

"Yes!"

"Funny. Okay, let's go onto the roof and give them a try."

It was hard to hold the animals and the megaphones while climbing the ladder, but Rafe used Dao's idea of putting them on their heads. They got to the roof and let the animals down.

"Okay, Dao," Rafe said. "Like this."

He held the small end of the megaphone to his mouth while holding the large end out.

"Helloooo! Helloooo! Can anyone hear me! We need help!"

Dao watched with delight. Rafe had her face the other direction. She put her megaphone to her mouth.

"Hello, people! Rafe says hi! Dao says hi! Come see us, okay?"

Rafe started calling again. The two of them shouted into the air, moving from one side of the roof to the other. They shouted until their throats were sore. Then they stopped to listen, but all they heard was the wind.

15

The Sound

Noisemaking became part of their daily routine, twice a day, right after the morning and afternoon exercise. At first it was fun, making all that noise, and they held out hope that somebody would hear them and answer back.

But after five days with not a sound in return, Rafe started to feel discouraged. He didn't want Dao to know, so he pretended to remain positive, sounding enthusiastic as they went up the ladder and then shouting with as much energy as he could muster. And when they were out of steam and had to stop, he would say, "Good session, Dao. I bet somebody will hear us tomorrow." Tomorrow, he always said. Tomorrow, tomorrow, tomorrow.

But maybe Dao, too, started to doubt. He thought he saw it in the way she avoided his eyes when they finished, and how afterward she would curl up on her air mattress with the cat, whispering to it in her language.

Yet, she too pretended to remain optimistic, perhaps for Rafe's sake. "I feel good," she would say. "I think tomorrow is now. We make noise for good people. People who give us bananas and popcorn."

One day, Rafe's voice gave out earlier than usual. He said, "Let's quit for today. The mist is rising anyway. We can't see farther than ten feet."

Dao came over to put her arm around him. "You do good noise, Rafe. We stay up?"

"Sure, if you like."

"Good. Sit. Today I tell *you* story."

"Okay." Rafe sat cross-legged on the roof. Dao followed. He looked out over the water. The mist made it feel as if they were sitting in a cloud.

"Once upon time is girl. Small. Strong."

"Gee, Dao, I wonder who that is."

"She live in high, high house. One, two, three, four, five, six, seven, eight, nine, ten, thirteen, fifteen houses up."

"You mean an apartment building?"

"Okay, yes. She live with Mama and Papa and sister and sister and brother and brother and sister."

"That *is* a big family."

"So big! She love family. They cook, they eat, they laugh, they fight, they play. All . . ."

She made a circular motion with her finger.

"All together?" Rafe said. "It sounds awfully nice."

"And then one day *this* happen." She pointed beyond the roof.

"The water?"

"Girl see from window. Big water coming. It fill street. It make cars and buses go up and down. It splish-splish on house. Going up fast, one, two, three, four up. She see people go out windows. Scary."

"I bet it was."

"Mama and Papa—"

She raised her hands and made a confused or maybe a scared face.

"They didn't know what to do," Rafe said.

"Yes. They look here; they look there. Use what? Use how? They give big ball to sister, horse to brother. Something to stay up on water."

"To float."

"And to the girl they give—"

"The air mattress. The bed."

"Maybe she gets best. She small. And now water goes fast. Right up to window. *Over* window! Splish-splish. Scream, ah! Cry, boo-hoo! Oh my, oh my. Papa and Mama say, 'Go!' Out window. 'Hold on!' they say."

"Oh, Dao."

"The girl, she so scared. No want to go."

"But she can't stay if the water's coming in."

"No, must go too. But first take cat. Mama, Papa say no cat. Girl say yes, yes."

"A very stubborn girl."

"She kiss Mama and Papa and hold cat and go. Splish-splish! She is riding water like wild horse. Up down up down up down."

"How long were you—I mean, was she floating before she found someone? How many days?"

"So many."

"And her mother and father? Her sisters and brothers? Did she ever see them?"

"See nothing. See nobody. All alone. And then she see boy." Her eyes filled with tears. "A boy name Rafe. Rafe her family now. Rafe and dog and cat. Her family."

Rafe felt his own eyes get wet. He didn't know what to say so he just stayed beside her. Buddy wandered over, wanting to be petted. He licked Dao's chin, making her giggle.

"I guess we better go back in," he said finally.

"Make noise one more time," said Dao. She stood up, put the bristol board megaphone to her mouth and began to shout.

"Weeee are heeere! Weeee are heeere! Weeee are heeere!"

Buddy was looking at her. His ears pricked up. He whimpered.

"What is it, Buddy?" asked Rafe.

The cat's back had gone stiff. Rafe stood on his tiptoes and looked. But he could see only mist.

"Something!" Dao said, standing up. "I hear *ding-dong.*"

Rafe strained to listen. *Was* it something? Yes, it was a bell. Faint but definitely there. Either somebody was ringing a bell or some debris was banging together.

"Quick," Rafe said. "Let's make more noise."

They raised their megaphones in the direction of the sound and started to shout. It didn't matter what they said or that their voices were so hoarse their throats burned.

Rafe put up his finger for them to be quiet. Again they listened.

The bell was ringing faster now—*ding, ding, ding, ding!* And it was a little less faint, a little closer.

"Do they really hear us?" Rafe asked. He looked out again. There was something just barely visible in the mist.

An outline. It looked like the prow of a ship or the edge of—what? He couldn't tell *what* it was.

And then he heard something else.

Voices.

He and Dao looked at one another. Their eyes were wide.

"People," she said in a hushed voice. "I hear people."

16

The Pile

It wasn't a ship or an island. It was a floating heap of refuse. Brown and yellow and green and blue. Stripes and squares and splotches. It was a gigantic raft made from rubber tires, old furniture, flattened cars, wooden beams and empty oil drums. Even though he couldn't see the end of it, Rafe could tell that it was moving with the water and was, therefore, not an island or the edge of land. And on it were, indeed, people. In the mist it was hard to tell how many.

"What they do?" asked Dao.

"I think they're waving at us."

"Okay! I wave too," Dao said, throwing her hands wildly in the air.

"But they're too far for us to ever reach. We can't steer the room, and I'm sure they can't steer that huge pile of junk they're on. We're going to miss them. They're going to float right by us."

"No, no, no. This no good. We go to people. We float on my bed."

"Both of us? And the animals too? Your air mattress won't hold us all up. But maybe you should go, Dao. You and the cat."

Dao frowned at him. She wagged her finger. "What, you silly boy? I go with my family or no."

Rafe looked at her. Did she really think of him as a brother? Did he think of her as a sister? Yes, he did. She really was his family now. But that was all the more reason he wanted her to go. She would have a better chance with more people.

"Dao, I still think—"

"Look!" she said, pointing.

Rafe stared into the mist. Something was happening on the heap. People were running about, pointing, talking. They were carrying something to the edge and lowering it into the water. It looked like a giant brown pencil.

A canoe! It must have been large because four people got in. And now they were paddling. They were paddling toward the room!

"You see too, Rafe?"

"I do see it!"

"What if they are bad, smelly pirates?"

"I can't be sure, but I don't think so. Look at Buddy and the cat. They're watching too. And they don't look afraid."

"You are right," Dao said. "Animals are smart cookies."

Together they stood and watched and waited. The canoe came toward them but slowly as the four paddlers had to fight the waves.

"This not sleep," Dao said. "It feels like sleep but is not."

Now Rafe could see the people in the boat. At the front was a woman with white streaks in her hair. She was giving instructions to the other three. They all paddled together, getting closer and closer.

"Ahoy there!" the woman called.

"Hi," said Dao. "Are you bad pirates?"

The young man behind the woman looked alarmed. "Have you seen pirates nearby?" he asked.

"No, not recently," Rafe called.

"They're a terrible problem," said the woman. "My name is Lucia. We live on that—well, we just call it the Pile. But it's home. We hope over time it's going to become more solid, like real ground. We hope it'll get covered with earth and then something might even grow on it. We've got seeds stored away."

"How many of you are there?" Rafe asked.

"Hmm, let's see. We took in a nice couple just yesterday. That makes two hundred and eighteen."

Rafe could hardly believe it. Compared to how many people he had seen since the new days began, two hundred and eighteen seemed like a giant city.

At that moment Dao couldn't contain herself. She began speaking quickly in Thai. Then she stopped. To Rafe's amazement a young woman at the back of the canoe spoke back to her in the same language. Dao practically jumped up and down with excitement as she started speaking again, her words flowing like music. Rafe could see how happy she was to be able to speak her own language again.

"We're wondering," said the older woman, "if you would like to join us? We've got a pretty good supply of food and water. Some of the people who used to be teachers are running classes, although attendance is voluntary. And we've got some games going, soccer and volleyball. We've made some musical instruments and there's a dance every few days. We even have a doctor, although not much medicine. But you don't have to join us if you don't want to. It's completely your choice."

"Just a minute," Rafe said. He turned to Dao. "What do you think?"

"We stay together? You and me and cat and dog?"

"It sounds like we can do what we want."

"Then I say . . . yes!"

Rafe turned back to the woman. "We'd like to join you. Thank you for asking us. Do we get in your boat?"

"Actually, you can stay where you are. We'll throw you a rope and pull you in. Then we can drag your room onto the Pile. We're trying to make it bigger, and it'll give you a place to sleep. Does that sound all right?"

Rafe looked at Dao. She nodded.

"Yes," Rafe said. "That sounds all right to us."

17
Remember

After they introduced themselves, the young man threw a rope. Rafe caught it. He spent some time looking for a way to anchor it before he finally tied it to the frame of his bed. Then he and Dao sat on the bed to weigh it down, the cat purring in Dao's lap, and Buddy getting his ears scratched by Rafe.

Buddy stretched forward and gave the cat a lick across her nose.

"Aw, see?" Dao said. "Buddy love cat."

They could feel when the rope grew taut and the room began to move slowly through the water. It must have been hard paddling and they could hear Lucia and and the others grunting with the effort. It took a long time for them to reach the Pile. It had a sort of dock made from a floating deck and the canoe pulled up beside it. Then some people came on the deck and grabbed the rope.

Rafe got the ladder and hung it from the window. "You go first," he said to Dao.

"Okay, Rafe. But first I do this."

She leaned forward and gave him a hug so hard that he almost fell over. Then she picked up the cat, *Conversations with a Rabbit* and the headless doll, all with one arm. She went out the window and down the ladder. Rafe watched. He saw the young woman crouch down to speak to her and pet the cat.

"I guess it's our turn, Buddy. You ready?"

Buddy did look a little nervous but he let Rafe pick him up. Rafe looked around his room and then he, too, went out and climbed down the ladder. It felt strange to put his feet onto the deck. Several people came around him, including Lucia.

"Welcome, Rafe. I'm sure you'll need a little time to get used to it here. But I bet you'll soon feel like you belong."

Rafe looked at her and suddenly he felt a tremendous pain in his heart. "I miss my parents," he said.

She put her arm around his shoulder. "I'm sure you do. I miss my son and my husband. Everybody here misses someone. We try to help one another."

"I haven't let myself think about them too much. Whenever I did, I had to push them out of my head. I just couldn't—I just couldn't—"

He started to cry. Lucia put her hand on his shoulder. "That's very understandable. You've been trying to survive. To be strong. For you and for Dao. That's what your parents would have wanted. They would have been so proud of you."

Her words made him cry harder, but she didn't move away. "I hope, Rafe, that you'll be able to take some time for yourself now. And for your feelings when you're ready. We've got a little place on the other side of the pile, with a bench and some flowers that the kids have made out of debris. We

just call it the Spot. It's a good place to sit, with someone or by yourself. I can show you. When you're up to it, you might want to spend some time remembering. Me, I don't want to forget the people I love. I try to remember little things about them, little moments. I say their names aloud. I think they would want us to remember them, don't you?"

Yes, Rafe thought, his parents would want that, but he couldn't manage to say anything. He and Lucia and Buddy started to walk, with Dao and the young woman and the cat ahead of them. They left the dock and now he could see better what the ground was made out of: old suitcases, iron balconies, piles of brick, plastic bins, all of it sort of crushed together. And farther on he could see little houses, huts really, made out of gypsum board and plywood and car doors. There were big funnels made out of scrap metal that must have been for gathering rainwater. The thought came to him that if there was one Pile, maybe there were more floating around the world. A few people said hello or patted him on the shoulder. He could see some kids playing together while a big drum was being used as a pot to cook over a fire. He could smell the stew, or whatever it was inside, and it made him realize how much he longed for a hot meal.

Two of the kids turned to look at him and Dao. They were small boys, no older than Dao, but they walked straight over without looking shy or worried. One of them leaned down to pet Buddy while the other stroked the cat.

"You want to come play?" the first one said.

"Maybe in a little while," Rafe answered. "I think we'll look around a bit."

"Okay. What's your dog's name?"

"Buddy."

The other boy said to Dao, "Hey, you've got a book with you."

"A good book," said Dao. "A girl and a rabbit."

"We've heard all of the kids' books that we have here on the Pile. Could you read it to us?"

"Sure. We start again, right, Rafe? From page number one."

Rafe looked at her smiling at him. Sure, why not start over again? This might be a book that he would never get to the end of. The boys nodded and ran back to the others.

"What do you think, Buddy?" Rafe said as they started walking again. "You think we'll be okay here?"

But Buddy wasn't listening, for something had distracted him. He was standing with his nose pointing and his ears back. Rafe stopped to see.

It was on a broken water fountain, something very small that was moving a little. Leaning down, Rafe saw that it was a moth. Not a butterfly but just an ordinary little moth with pale yellow wings. It was opening and closing its wings in the sunshine.

Dao had come up beside him and she was looking at it too.

"Is real?" she whispered.

"Yes, it's real."

"That," she began, "that . . ."

He put his hand in hers. "That," he said, "is the most beautiful thing I've ever seen."

Acknowledgments

Gratitude to Lynne Missen, to Tara Walker, to John Martz for his splendid design, and to Peter Phillips and everyone at Tundra Books. Thank you to Jon McNaught for his illustrations; you've made a long-time fan very happy. And a special thanks to all the school kids who heard the first chapter and wanted to know more.

CARY FAGAN's numerous kids' books include *The Collected Works of Gretchen Oyster* (a JLG selection), the Kaspar Snit novels, and the Wolfie & Fly chapter books. His picture books include *King Mouse* (finalist for the Governor General's Award) and *Bear Wants to Sing*. Cary has received the Vicky Metcalf Award for Literature for Young People for his body of work. He lives in Toronto.

JON McNAUGHT draws comics, and works as an illustrator, printmaker and lecturer. He is the author of several comic books including *Kingdom* (2018), and *Dockwood*, which was the winner of the Angoulême Prix Révélation award in 2012. He lives in London, UK.